The Lost Tomb of INCHAZARR

Written by Stella Santa Cruz

Illustrated by Ian Forss

Contents

Meet the Characters

Monty

A nine-year-old smuggling mastermind.

Bazz

Monty's friend.

Rachel

Monty's friend.

Señor Oswaldo

Monty, Bazz and Rachel's Bolivian guide.

Señor Hernandez

A Bolivian antique dealer.

Dear Reader

I've always wanted to visit Bolivia – but I'd rather be a tourist there, as I don't think I'd make a very good evil mastermind. Here's a fictional story about some evil masterminds with the perfect disguises – they're kids! Who would believe that?

Stella Santa Cruz
Author

The Region

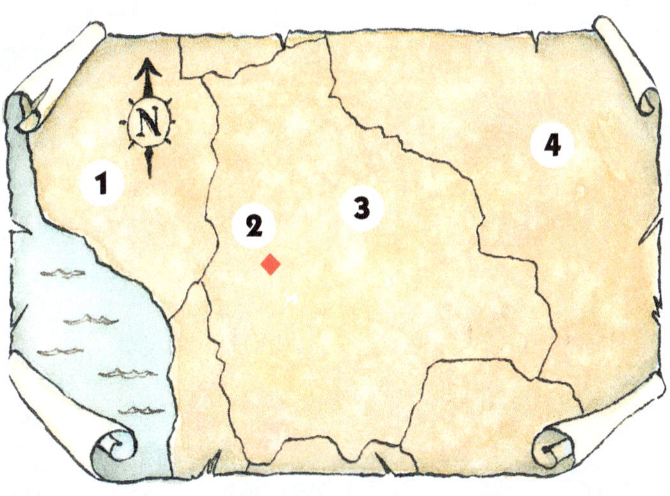

1. Peru
2. La Paz
3. Bolivia
4. Brazil

1 Prologue

PLEASED TO MEET YOU!

Monty's my name. Here's my card.

Don't let anyone catch you with that. I'm wanted in 59 countries!

It's true that most smuggling masterminds are older than me. Nine is a lot younger than many of those who smuggle art treasures. But being nine is the perfect disguise.

But you know, I'm not only a smuggling mastermind.

I'm also an expert on the Incas of South America and the Official Whiz-Kid for the year.

When you win on the TV show *Who Wants To Be A Whiz-Kid?*, you can choose any prize you want. After answering ten questions in a row on ancient Incan art treasures, I chose my perfect prize. It was a three-week trip to Bolivia with my best friends, Bazz and Rachel.

My favourite book is *The Lost Tomb of Inchazarr.* It's about an explorer called Diaz. He stumbled upon a huge Incan treasure trove in the tomb of a king called Inchazarr. Diaz fell sick with a strange jungle illness. Before he died, he wrote about Inchazarr's treasure, but no one ever found it. The treasure was lost!

But I have plans for the lost tomb of Inchazarr. Read on. I might let you in on my secrets!

2 Señor Oswaldo

So there I was, getting off a plane at La Paz Airport with Bazz and Rachel. For a moment, I forgot all about my clever plan. We gazed in awe at the high mountain that rose up behind the city.

A man in a bright-blue suit waited at the bottom of the steps. He had muscles the size of footballs, and waved a sign as people walked past.

"Mr Minty Mr Buzz Miss Rachet," read the sign.

"I'm Monty!" I said. "But you can call me 'Boss'. And this is Bazz and Rachel."

The man smiled.

"Welcome, Señor Boss. *Bienvenido a Bolivia*!" He smiled at Bazz and Rachel, too. "Welcome Señor Bazz and Señorita Rachel! *Bienvenido*!"

"Who are you, Señor?" I asked.

The man shook my hand. "I am Señor Oswaldo, your guide. The Whiz-Kid show has asked me to look after you and your friends while you are in our beautiful country."

"Great!" I said. "You can help us find the lost tomb of Inchazarr."

Oswaldo laughed and picked up our bags. "That's just a story," he chortled. "There is no lost tomb."

Oswaldo led us through the airport.

"Come on," he said, heading towards a battered old Cadillac outside. "La Paz awaits!"

I could tell he'd make a very good get-away driver!

3 A Life of Luxury

While Bazz, Rachel and I went up to our hotel room, Oswaldo sat himself and his blue suit down in the lobby. He flicked through *El Diario*, the city's newspaper, and found the crossword.

Upstairs, we couldn't believe our eyes. We'd never been in a triple luxury room!

Chocolates lay on all the pillows. There were bowls of fruit. There was a plasma TV with a hundred channels. Even the bathroom had a TV and a telephone!

There were three pairs of slippers under the beds. There were free video games on the desk. There were mobile phones for us to use. Everything had a remote control – the TV, the lights, the stereo, the curtains, even the windows – and there was a huge menu of snacks by the phone.

My friends and I flopped on our beds.

"If my plan works, we'll have to get used to this luxury," I said.

"Your plan?" said Bazz and Rachel.

It was time to let them into the secret. I explained why I had really chosen to come to Bolivia.

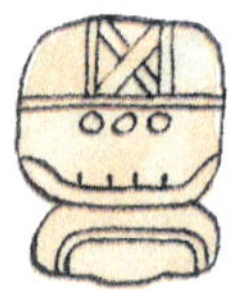

Later, we all rode the lift to the lobby. There, we found Oswaldo asleep, pen in hand, and the crossword in his lap.

I nudged him.

"Collasuyu," I said.

"*Que*?" yawned Oswaldo.

"Six down," I explained. "Ancient Incan province."

"Aha!" said Oswaldo, looking at his crossword. "I was just about to write that … How is your room, Boss?"

"Cool, thanks. But we'd like to go out."

"Where to?" asked Oswaldo. "A toy shop? Minigolf? A movie? Or perhaps the zoo?"

I grinned. So far, my disguise as a good nine-year-old was working fine. "The local market, please."

Oswaldo was surprised. "Well, OK," he said. "What do you want to see? Spices? Crafts? Food?"

"Antiques!" I said.

"*Antigüedades*?" said Oswaldo. "Are you sure?"

"Oh, yes," I nodded.

"We're sure!" agreed Bazz and Rachel. They were excited at the thought of becoming assistant art treasure smuggling masterminds.

Oswaldo looked at us. "OK!" he said, shrugging his shoulders. "*Vayamos*! Let's go!"

4 Antique Treasures

Oswaldo could finally rest his weary feet. After three hours of scouring dozens of market shops, I had found what I wanted.

"It's a real Incan treasure," hissed the shopkeeper, Señor Hernandez. His eyes darted from side to side.

I looked at the pottery urn that Señor Hernandez was referring to.

"I should not be selling that," added Hernandez, tapping his nose. "It is forbidden to sell ancient Incan art treasures. But for the right price, I may be able to part with it."

Oswaldo filled the doorway to the shop. He too was glancing from side to side. It would not do for the winner of *Who Wants To Be A Whiz-Kid?* to be caught smuggling art treasures while in his care.

Meanwhile, Bazz and Rachel poked around the shop, looking.

"The right price?" I sniffed. "That would be a dollar."

"*Tengo miedo no*!" chuckled the shopkeeper, shaking his head. "I'm afraid not. This relic is thousands of years old. It was secretly smuggled to La Paz from the lost tomb of Inchazarr itself."

"It's a fake," I replied, with a smile. "The pattern is not at all like those in the lost tomb of Inchazarr. The colours are not right. And the pottery style is from a different age."

Señor Hernandez waved his arms.

"Pssst, Monty!" hissed Rachel. "What about this?" She pointed into an old cabinet.

"Hmm," I said, seeing something that was not a fake. "Now, that looks good."

"Aha!" said the shopkeeper, looking even shiftier. "The *señorita* has good eyes! A real stone carving of Pachamama, the earth goddess. It was lost for centuries in a site which really is the lost tomb of Inchazarr! Only my cousin's family knows where it is. This is extremely rare. It would be very illegal for me to sell such a national art treasure to you. Unless ..."

Oswaldo shuffled in the doorway. He had seen a policeman strolling down the street. It looked like he was wishing his suit wasn't quite so blue or so bright.

"Señor Boss," he warned, "this is not a good idea. Are you sure you wouldn't rather go minigolfing?"

Bazz peered under Oswaldo's arm. "He's right, Monty," he said. "There's a policeman out there."

It was time to go.

I smiled at the shopkeeper. "We'll be back, Señor Hernandez. If your cousin has any other art treasures, I'd like to see them."

The shopkeeper nodded. "Shall we say three o'clock tomorrow?"

5 In the Cadillac

We bounced towards the hotel in the back of Oswaldo's old car.

Suddenly, Bazz sat up.

"Oswaldo, I forgot my sunglasses!" he said. "Can we go back to the antique shop, please?"

Oswaldo swung the Cadillac in a U-turn. Cars tooted behind us like a Bolivian brass band.

"No problem," he said. Soon, we were back in the maze of streets.

“There he is,” whispered Rachel. She pointed to the shopkeeper walking down the street. We watched as he checked behind himself, then went into a doorway in the next block.

“Now we know where to go,” I smiled.

“Found them!” cried Bazz, with a loud

laugh. "They were on my head the whole time!"

Oswaldo shrugged. The Cadillac swerved again and went back to the main road.

"Where to now, *amigos*?" beamed Oswaldo.

"Let's go Bolivian minigolfing," I suggested.

Even nine-year-old art-treasure smuggling masterminds and their assistants need to have some fun!

After losing five rounds of minigolf, Oswaldo was relieved to drop us back at the hotel.

"So, I shall pick you up tomorrow for your three o'clock 'appointment'," he said, from the driver's seat.

"Make it earlier," I said, with a crafty look. "We may have a two o'clock appointment as well."

6 The Game's Up!

At exactly *two* o'clock the next day, we loudly thumped on the door of a familiar building.

Señor Hernandez and his cousin and his cousin's wife and his cousin's nine-year-old twin boys, Felix and Fuego, leapt up from their table and stared at us.

A huge blue shadow stood behind us. We stood with our arms folded.

I stepped forward.

"The game's up!" I growled, pointing at the tiny sculptures and carvings on the table. "Your antique smuggling ring is about to be smashed!"

Felix and Fuego gasped.

"*Contrabando*?" they said. "Smuggling?"

“You should be ashamed of yourselves,” I continued. “Selling Incan art treasures! It’s against the law!”

Señor Hernandez held out his hands to plead with me. His eyes kept darting to Oswaldo. I could tell he thought the man in the blue suit looked far too big to tackle.

“But these things are not really from the lost tomb of Inchazarr! My cousin Miguel and his wife Zuma are poor farmers,” he said. Miguel and Zuma nodded their heads. “They found these when they were planting corn in their fields. I agreed to help them.”

I sighed, and shook my head. “I’ll have to report you to the police.”

I punched a number into the mobile phone I’d brought from the hotel.

Señor Hernandez, Miguel, Zuma, Felix and Fuego all started to talk in Spanish, and point at each other angrily.

I raised a finger. It was time to put the next piece of my plan into action.

"Unless …" I said, snapping the phone shut.

"*Si*?" said the twins.

oOo

Half an hour later, Oswaldo grinned and sipped his coffee. "No, I couldn't," he said, waving away another slice of Zuma's best chocolate cake.

Señor Hernandez put down the phone, and rubbed his hands.

"All OK, Boss!" he said. "We start tomorrow." He clapped me on the back.

"Cool," I said. I was working my way through a sack of dirt-covered figurines that Miguel had proudly brought out from the kitchen.

Bazz and Rachel took notes as I explained my plan.

"With my knowledge of Incan treasures," I began, "we can make perfect copies of these treasures – much better than the fakes that Señor Hernandez has in his shop."

"The fake factory will start tomorrow," repeated Señor Hernandez, "under your expert eyes."

"You have indeed dug up a treasure trove in your corn fields. We shall pretend it really is the lost tomb of Inchazarr," I said. "No one will know. And perhaps it really is ..."

“But how will we sell these perfect copies?” asked Felix.

“Uncle Hernandez won’t be able to sell more than one or two in his shop,” added Fuego.

“That’s where you two come in,” I said. “I know all the big collectors of Incan treasures. I’ll say I have met two poor Bolivian boys who have found Inchazarr’s lost tomb!”

“So we sell the perfect forgeries to greedy collectors. The originals stay in Bolivia.

We can give them to a museum later!" exclaimed Oswaldo. "I like the plan, Boss!"

"*Eso es extra brillante*!" agreed Felix and Fuego. "It's extra brilliant!"

"Señor Monty," said the twins, shaking my hand warmly. "This is the start of a wonderful friendship!"

I smiled. My new Bolivian partners and I were going to be rich – as well as keeping Incan treasures in Bolivia, where they belonged!

"Now, how about we all head to the hotel?" I said. "I know a cool Cadillac that's going that way. And there's great room service, too!"

The nine members of Bolivia's newest art treasure smuggling and forgery ring cheered. We all headed for the door.

o0o

Now, I ask you! What is wrong with that? I think we are doing the right thing. Don't you agree?

Have you still got my card? Oh, and by the way, if you've found any art treasures lately, why not give me a call?

THE END